John Burningham

BORKA

THE ADVENTURES OF A GOOSE
WITH NO FEATHERS

RED FOX

For Helen

Some other picture books by John Burningham

Aldo	*Mr Gumpy's Motor Car*
Avocado Baby	*Mr Gumpy's Outing*
Cloudland	*Oi! Get Off*
Come Away From the Water, Shirley	*Our Train*
	Picnic
Courtney	*The Shopping Basket*
Edwardo, the Horriblest Boy in the Whole Wide World	*Simp*
	Time to Get Out of the Bath, Shirley
Granpa	
Harquin	*Trubloff*
Humbert	*Tug of War*
Husherbye	*Whadayamean*
John Patrick Norman McHennessy	*Where's Julius*
The Magic Bed	*Would You Rather?*

BORKA: THE ADVENTURES OF A GOOSE WITH NO FEATHERS
A RED FOX BOOK 978 0 099 40067 7

First published in Great Britain by Jonathan Cape, an imprint of Random House Children's Publishers UK
A Random House Group Company

Jonathan Cape edition published 1963
Red Fox edition first published 1992
This anniversary edition published 2013

1 3 5 7 9 10 8 6 4 2

Copyright © John Burningham, 1963

The right of John Burningham to be identified as the author of this work has been asserted
in accordance with the Copyright, Designs and Patents Act 1988.

All rights reserved. No part of this publication may be reproduced, stored in a retrieval system, or transmitted in any form or by any means,
electronic, mechanical, photocopying, recording or otherwise, without the prior permission of the publishers.

Red Fox Books are published by Random House Children's Publishers UK, 61–63 Uxbridge Road, London W5 5SA

www.randomhousechildrens.co.uk   www.randomhouse.co.uk

Addresses for companies within The Random House Group Limited can be found at: www.randomhouse.co.uk/offices.htm

THE RANDOM HOUSE GROUP Limited Reg. No. 954009

A CIP catalogue record for this book is available from the British Library.

Printed in China

MIX
Paper from
responsible sources
FSC
www.fsc.org
FSC® C104723

The Random House Group Limited supports the Forest Stewardship Council® (FSC®), the leading international
forest-certification organisation. Our books carrying the FSC label are printed on FSC®-certified paper. FSC is the
only forest-certification scheme supported by the leading environmental organisations, including Greenpeace.
Our paper procurement policy can be found at www.randomhouse.co.uk/environment

Once upon a time there were two geese called Mr and Mrs Plumpster.

They lived on a deserted piece of marshland near the East Coast of England, where their ancestors had once lived many years before. There they built their nest and laid their eggs.

Each spring the Plumpsters came back to the marshes and mended their nest. Then Mrs Plumpster settled down to lay her eggs, and Mr Plumpster kept guard.

He hissed at anything that came near the nest.
  Sometimes he hissed even if there was nothing in sight.
It made him feel important.

Then the eggs began to hatch. One fine spring morning there were six baby Plumpsters in the nest.

Mr Plumpster was delighted, and he invited his friends round to celebrate.
  The young geese were given names. They were

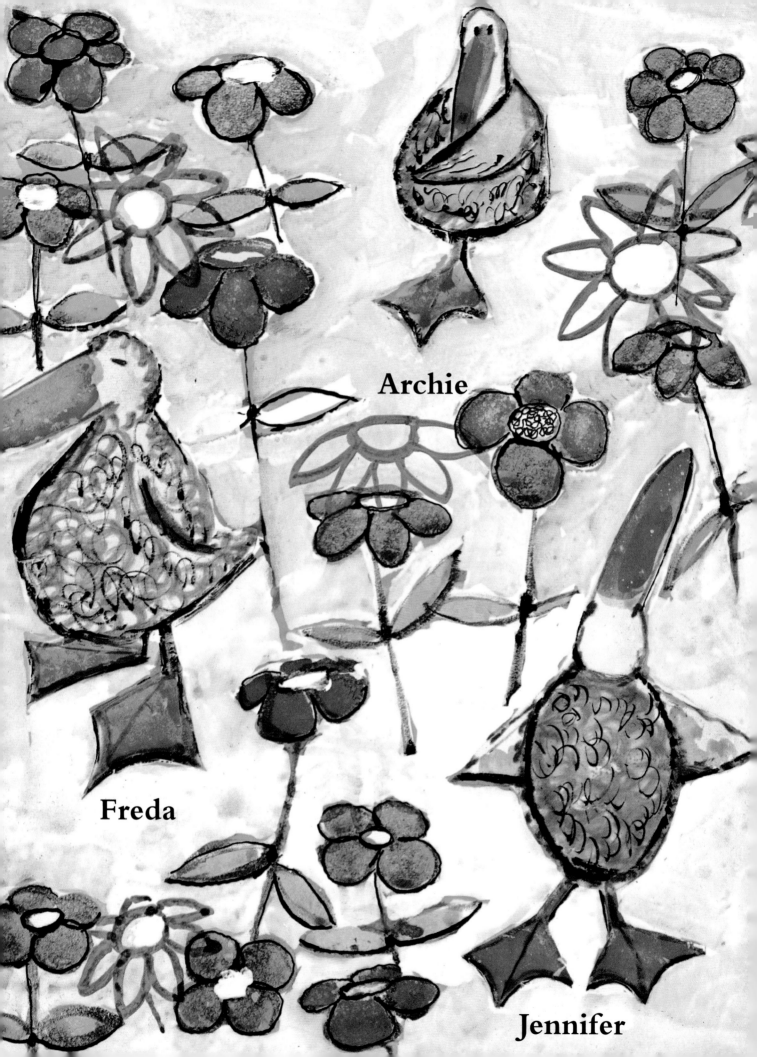

Archie

Freda

Jennifer

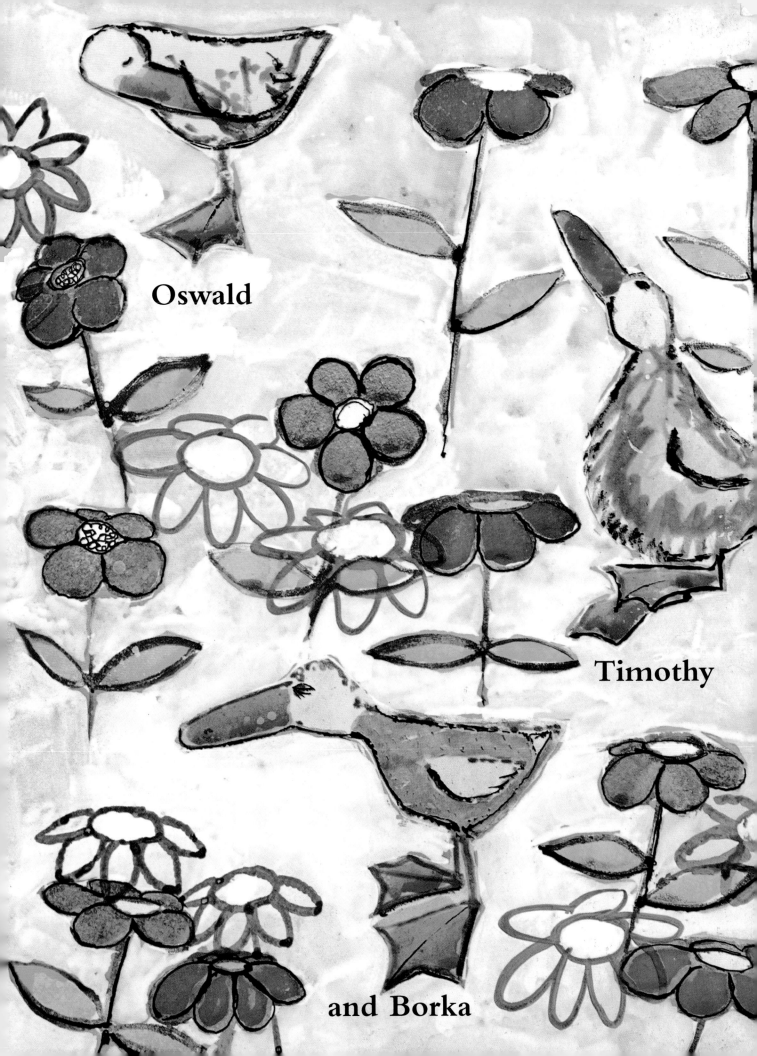

Oswald

Timothy

and Borka

Now all geese look very much alike when they are young, but right from the start there was something odd about Borka. Borka had a beak, wings, and webbed feet like all her brothers and sisters, but she did not have any feathers.

Mr and Mrs Plumpster were very worried about this. They called in the doctor goose who examined Borka carefully. He said there was nothing wrong with her except that she did not have any feathers. "A most unusual case," he went on, and he thought for a long while. Then he told Mrs Plumpster that there was only one thing to do. She must knit some feathers for Borka.

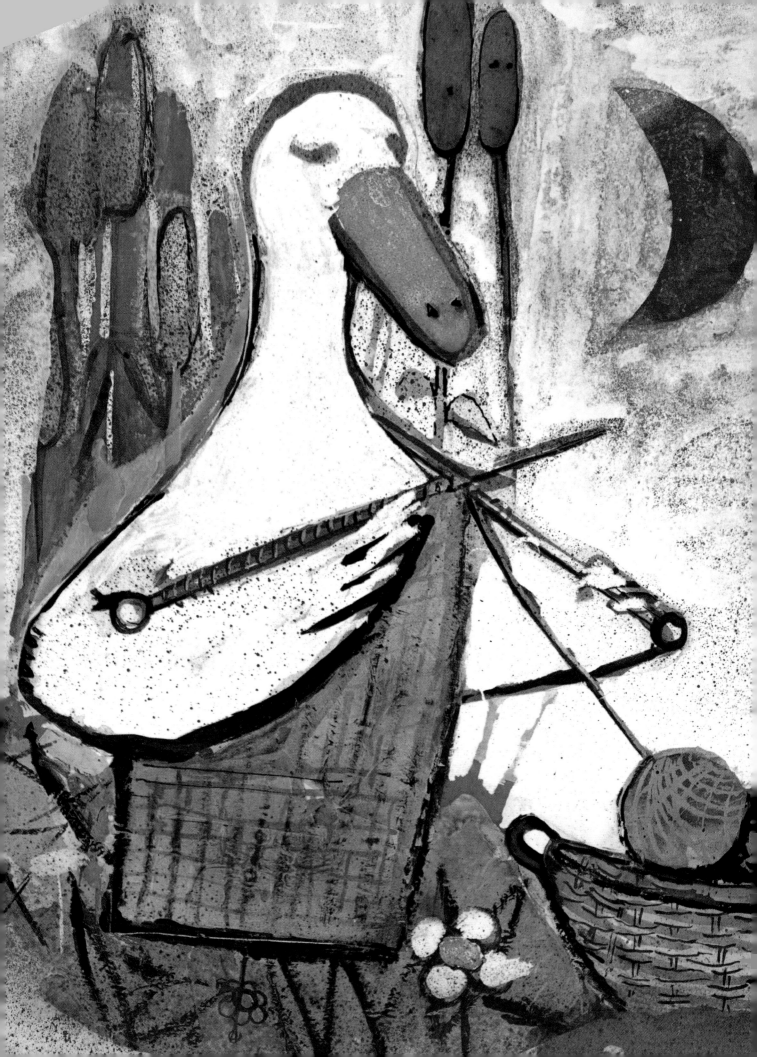

So Mrs Plumpster got out her knitting needles and
set to work. Of course she could not knit real
feathers, but she made a kind of grey woollen jersey
as much like feathers as she could.
   When she had finished, she called Borka
and tried it on her. Borka was delighted,
and flapped around with joy, because
she had always been chilly at night.

She went and showed the other young geese, but they just laughed at her. This made her very unhappy and she went into a patch of tall reeds and cried.

Now by this time the other young geese were learning to fly and to swim properly. But Borka did not like joining in because the others teased her, and so she got very behind with her lessons.

Nobody noticed that she was not attending. Mr and Mrs Plumpster were far too busy. Borka did try to learn to swim, but whenever she went into the water, her jersey took such a long time to dry afterwards that she soon gave up.

By now the summer was almost over. The weather was getting cooler and the geese were becoming restless. At this time of year they always went to a warmer land where it was easier to find food.

The Plumpsters began getting ready to leave. They covered their nest with twigs and rushes to keep it safe through the stormy winter.

Then one day it became really cold and wet.

The geese shivered, and knew it was time for them to go. They chose one wise old goose to lead them and they all flew away.

But Borka did not go. She could not fly. Instead she went and hid, and watched them leave. Nobody noticed that she was missing. They were all too busy thinking of the journey ahead. As the geese disappeared into the grey sky, tears trickled down Borka's beak.

She did not know what to do.

It was drizzling, and she wandered off, hoping to find a dry place for the night. It was already getting dark when she came to a line of boats moored in the estuary. Borka chose one that had no lights on board, and she walked up the gangplank.

She was just going down into the hold of the boat when
there was a loud bark. A dog came rushing out, which
gave Borka a terrible fright. But the dog, seeing it was
only a goose, stopped barking and introduced himself.
He was called Fowler.

Borka explained that she only wanted to stay under
cover for the night, so Fowler showed her into a part of
the hold where there were some old sacks for her to lie
on. She was so tired that she fell asleep almost at once.

Now the boat, which was called the *Crombie*, belonged to Captain McAllister. Late that night he and his mate, whose name was Fred, came back, and they decided to sail early in the morning before it was light. Fowler forgot all about Borka, who was still asleep in the hold.

It was not until they were well on their way that he remembered, and told the Captain.

"Well, well!" said Captain McAllister.

"A goose on board! She'll have to work her passage if she's coming with us to London."

Borka was soon very
friendly with the
Captain, Fred and, of
course, with Fowler.
She coiled pieces of
rope with her beak,
picked up crumbs
from the floor and
helped in any
way she could.

In return she
was given
plenty of
good food.

At last the *Crombie* steamed into the Thames and they were nearing London. Captain McAllister began to wonder what to do with Borka when they got there.

He decided to leave her in Kew Gardens, which is a large park where lots of geese live all the year round.

When they came to the place where the river flows past Kew Gardens, Captain McAllister lifted Borka over the railings and put her with the other geese. She was sorry to say goodbye to her friends but they promised to come and visit her on their next trip to London.

The geese at Kew did not mind that Borka had no
feathers. There were already so many strange kinds of
birds in the gardens. Nobody laughed at her grey
woollen jersey and all the geese were very friendly,
especially one called Ferdinand. Ferdinand cared for
Borka and taught her to swim really well. She is still
living there happily and whenever Captain McAllister and
Fred and Fowler come to London they call in to see her.

So if you are in Kew Gardens at any time and you see a goose who looks somehow different from the others – it might well be Borka.